CHRIS HIGHAM

Chris Higham, the artist who has illustrated this exciting new book in the *Award Colour Classics* series, was born in Kingston-upon-Thames in 1944. After studying for several years at Epsom Art School in Surrey, he worked for Venture Studio for three years before becoming a freelance illustrator. Since then, he has illustrated many books and magazines.

ISBN 0 86163 069 6

Award Publications Limited 1982
Spring House, Spring Place
London NW5, England

© 1982 Victoria House Publishing

Printed in Belgium

ROBIN HOOD

Retold by Jane Carruth

AWARD PUBLICATIONS — LONDON

Robin Hood the outlaw

MORE THAN eight hundred years ago there was a king of England called Richard the Lionheart. Richard went abroad for long periods of time to fight great battles and while he was away, the land was ruled by his brother, Prince John.

John was a cruel and tyrannical man and he appointed men just like himself to positions of power throughout the country. One of his favourites was the Sheriff of Nottingham. Thirsty for riches and power, the Sheriff controlled Nottinghamshire with an iron hand. He burdened the poor peasants with harsh taxes and if they could not pay, his soldiers would turn them out of their homes and farms.

One man stood up against the Sheriff. He was the Saxon Earl of Huntingdonshire. He was such a thorn in the Sheriff's flesh that Prince John outlawed him. The Earl set up camp in a secret glade in the heart of a huge forest and gathered around him a band of men dedicated to fighting injustice and determined to do whatever they could to help the peasants.

The forest was Sherwood Forest and the earl came to be known as Robin Hood.

The highway to Nottingham Town ran through the forest, and it was on this road that Robin and his men carried out some of their most daring exploits.

No fat Norman baron or overfed merchant or pompous man of law was safe from Robin. Time and again, with cheerful courtesy, he and his bold men dressed in Lincoln green robbed the rich of their money-bags. But the gold they took was not just for themselves. Most of it was given to the poor folk of the surrounding countryside who suffered so cruelly under the Normans.

Robin was one of the best swordsmen in the land and his fame as an archer was widespread. No one could match his gift of leadership, his courage and his cheerfulness.

The Sheriff hated and feared him. He longed to capture Robin, and see him hang from his gallows! Over and over again, he vowed that he would capture the Saxon outlaw, dead or alive! But Robin had many friends who were determined that come what may, the Sheriff would never succeed. One of them was his cousin, Will Gamwell, son of Squire Roger Gamwell of Gamwell Hall.

It was at the Hall that Robin had met and fallen in love with the gentle Maid Marian. It was she who had given him the fine forester's horn which he used to summon his merry men. And now, as Robin, Will and Marian stood in the great hall of Gamwell, she was trying to stop him going on yet another reckless adventure.

"Will," she cried, turning to Robin's cousin, "please try and make Robin understand the terrible risks . . ."

"Why, I had hoped to take Will along with me to Nottingham," laughed Robin. "What do you say, cousin? Shall we beard the Sheriff in his den?"

"Certainly!" said Will. "But not dressed as we are. That Lincoln green suit you wear so boldly would surely attract unwelcome attention."

"We'll disguise ourselves," cried Robin. "I'll wear a black patch over one eye. And you must smear that handsome face of yours all over with soot. We shall be the two most disreputable looking rascals who ever attended Nottingham Fair, I promise you."

Marian shrugged helplessly and went off to find the oldest clothes in the Hall. An hour later even she had to agree that Robin and Will had done a good job. Robin's doublet was patched at the elbows and ripped down one side. His hose had once been brown but had been darned so often that they were now an assortment of multi-coloured wools. He had wrapped sackcloth round his feet and tied it round with twine. The patch on his eye gave him a sinister appearance. Will was dressed much the same and there was so much soot on his face that he looked as if he had just climbed a chimney.

Not even his closest friends would have recognised Robin, as he passed through the town's gates and headed for the market-square. Will was close behind him and his eyes darted back and forth keeping a sharp look out for the Sheriff's men.

The square was crowded. The cries of the stall-holders mingled with the delighted shouts of the townspeople and the music of wandering minstrels. Groups of Morris men danced around in colourful costumes. The whole square was alive with colour and the sounds of people being happy: and Robin and Will merrily joined in the fun.

Soon came the announcement that Robin had been waiting for; the archery contest was about to begin in the square.

Robin's eyes sparkled when he heard this.

"Come, Will," he cried, taking hold of his cousin's arm. "Let us go and see for ourselves how the Norman archers fare against the yeomen!"

By the time Robin and Will arrived at the square where the contest was to be held, a large crowd had already gathered around the archers.

As they watched, several of the contestants were quickly eliminated when their arrows completely missed the small, inner black circle which had been painted on the butt.

"If only I had a bow and a quiver of arrows," Robin remarked in a loud voice,

"I would soon try my luck against the Sheriff's men!"

He had no sooner spoken than a hefty Saxon thrust his own longbow into Robin's hand.

"Shoot, man!" he urged. "Show these proud Normans what you can do!"

With a merry twinkle in his eyes, Robin indicated that he wished to join the contestants. There was a murmur of protest from the foresters whose leader was expected to win the coveted prize money-belt. But the lusty yeomen among the crowd roared their approval of Robin's request. And he stepped forward and raised his bow.

A hush fell upon the onlookers as they considered the new challenger. "Can a man with a patch over one eye hope to shoot straight?" one plump farmer's wife asked her husband.

"Hush, woman," the farmer exclaimed. "Even with one eye a Saxon is worth ten Normans."

Robin smiled to himself as he overheard this remark. Then he took careful aim and let fly his arrow. It struck the very centre of the small black circle.

"The winner!" yelled some of the crowd.

"You shout too soon!" snapped the leader of the foresters. "I have not yet had my turn."

With an air of supreme confidence he fitted his arrow into the bow and let fly. To his bitter disappointment his arrow just missed the centre of the target, and he turned on his heel, a grim scowl on his thin face.

The roar from the Saxons in the crowd could be heard all over Nottingham as Robin was declared the winner of the contest. Several sturdy yeomen surrounded him and carried him shoulder high to a rough platform on which sat the judge.

Robin grinned cheerfully as he accepted the prize-belt. What a story he would have to tell Maid Marian when he next saw her! But his moment of triumph was short-lived.

Some of the foresters, furious that the valuable prize should have gone to a mere tinker, began striking out with their staves. Taken by surprise, Robin and Will were beaten about the head and knocked to the ground.

A number of stout-hearted Saxons rushed to their rescue and a fierce battle of quarterstaffs and cudgels was soon in progress.

Struggling to their feet, Robin and his cousin plunged into the thick of the fighting giving as good as they got.

Suddenly someone shouted, "Here comes the Sheriff!"

"Give this to the Sheriff," cried one old woman as she threw a ripe orange which hit one of the foresters square in the face.

"It's the hangman's rope for us if we are caught here," Will grunted to Robin, clumping an overfed Norman in the stomach with his staff. "Let's get out of here while we can."

They slipped through the jostling crowds unnoticed and, much to Will's relief, soon reached the forest in safety.

When Gamwell Hall came into view, Robin exclaimed, "The colour will surely rush to Marian's face when we tell her of our outing!"

"Never put yourself at such risk again," Will protested soberly.

But Robin only laughed. "If my gentle Marian can not persuade me to give such a promise, Will, shall I give it to you?"

And Will, as they crossed the drawbridge and entered the house, knew the answer only too well.

Robin Hood and Little John

I T WAS not advisable for Robin to stay more than a night or two at Gamwell Hall so his visits were always brief.

And, in fact, he was never completely happy until he was back in the beautiful greenwood glade among his merry men. One day, as he was returning from the Hall, he saw on the other bank of a stream a man of most unusual size.

This giant of a man was heading for a felled tree-trunk which had been placed across the stream and served as a bridge.

Robin always used this bridge to reach his camp, so he quickened his steps accordingly, determined to reach the stream before the giant. The big man on the opposite bank lengthened his stride, almost as if he had read Robin's mind.

Both men reached the bridge almost exactly at the same moment.

"Give way!" roared the giant, shaking a huge staff at Robin. "I claim the right to be the first to cross!"

Robin threw back his head and laughed.

"You bray like an ass!" he shouted. "Give way, you insolent fellow. I intend to be the first to cross!" And he drew an arrow from his quiver.

"Coward!" taunted the giant. "Shoot me down, would you? Why not cut yourself a staff and fight it out like a man and not the miserable shrimp you are?"

Not knowing whether to be amused or angry, Robin went back up the bank and cut himself a stout stick from one of the oak trees.

"I'll fight you on your own terms, on the bridge itself," he declared in a ringing voice. "Whoever is the first to fall into the water has lost the contest."

The two men advanced to meet each other on the slender bridge. And, after a flourish or two, the battle began in earnest.

The giant aimed a blow at Robin's head which, if it had found its mark, would

have put an end to his fighting for many a day. But the outlaw skilfully parried it and, in his turn, brought down his oak staff on the stranger's massive shoulders. The blow would have sent any ordinary man flying through the air, but the giant merely shook his head and redoubled his own blows.

Suddenly, the huge man let out a fierce roar as if in warning. Such a storm of blows followed his war-like cry, many of them finding their mark, that Robin was almost knocked off his feet.

He began to sway and, in an effort to keep his balance, dropped his staff. Then with a shout of dismay he toppled, head first, into the stream.

The stream was fast-running and deep and Robin Hood hit the water with a tremendous splash. His adversary gave a bellow of triumph and crossed to the far bank. When Robin's head bobbed into sight, the giant pretended not to notice and kept up his indifference when Robin waded to the bank and stood before him.

"Well done!" said Robin Hood, as he squeezed some of the water out of his dripping tunic. "It was a fairly fought fight and the better man won in the end!"

"What, you bear me no malice?" exclaimed the giant. "You're a grand wee fighting cock, I'll give you that!"

"Why should I?" returned Robin. "You're a fellow after my own heart and one I would gladly have at my side in any battle. What's your name?"

"That's no business of yours," retorted the stranger. "But I'll tell you for all that. It's John Little – a strange name for a man of my size, you'll admit. And if you want to know where I am going, well, to be frank with you, I'm in two minds. It could be Nottingham Town or it could be York!"

"Why not stay here in Sherwood Forest?" suggested Robin. "Join me and

my men! Robin Hood is my name and I have made my home here along with some others who have fallen foul of Prince John. Here we shall stay until the proud Prince is put in his place. My lads are as brave as they come." Robin spoke with a note of pride in his voice.

"I've heard of you," admitted the giant somewhat grudgingly. "Is it true that with a blast on that horn of yours that dangles from your neck, you can summon your men from all parts of the forest?" John Little asked with a gleam in his eye.

"True enough," said Robin. And to prove it he raised the horn to his lips. The air was not rent with a sharp blast as Robin expected. Instead, a thin warble and a stream of water spluttered from the horn.

The two men burst out laughing and Robin shook the remaining water out of the horn and tried again.

Almost before the sound of his horn had died away, out of the wood ran several men, all dressed in Lincoln green.

"This is John Little," said Robin. "He beat me in a fair fight and threw me in the stream."

At this, several of the men made as if to set about John, who grasped his huge staff and raised it menacingly.

"No, no, let him be!" exclaimed Robin. "If he is willing, and you agree, I propose we make him a member of our company."

The black looks directed at John changed to smiles, and satisfied, Robin Hood led his band back to their secret greenwood glade.

According to their custom, no sooner were they back at camp than Robin con-sulted his men regarding a new name for their latest recruit.

"What shall it be?" Robin asked the company. "The name should perhaps indicate something of John Little's immense size!"

There was silence for a moment. Then Much-the-Miller's son called out, "Why not Little John?"

His suggestion was greeted with a gust of laughter but, to the surprise of everyone, the giant nodded. "That is good

enough for me," he said. "And it's a name that won't easily slip from memory, being so like my own."

The men formed a half circle in front of the famous Greenwood Tree – a great spreading oak intertwined with ivy – and Robin Hood, in a solemn voice, announced that the ceremony of re-christening John was about to begin.

Much-the-Miller's son filled Robin's horn with wine and stretching upwards, Robin managed to pour some of it over John's head.

"I christen thee Little John!" he cried. "May your service in our company be an honourable and right merry one!"

Little John was then given an outfit of Lincoln green and preparations for a feast were put in hand.

That night, under the greenwood trees, there was a great banquet followed by merry-making such as the outlaws had not enjoyed for some time. And the loudest voice of all that was raised in song and ballad was that of Robin Hood's newest recruit, Little John!

A knight in distress

LITTLE JOHN soon became one of Robin Hood's most trusted lieutenants. And it was he, together with his companions, Will Gamwell and Much-the-Miller's son who, one morning, came upon the shabbiest looking knight they had ever seen. His cloak was travel-stained and threadbare, his shoulders were hunched dejectedly and the nag upon which he sat seemed almost as weary and dispirited as its master.

The three outlaws watched the knight's slow progress along the highroad for a while. Then Little John said, "Robin told us to find a guest for dinner to enliven the meal. Shall we make do with that sad spectacle?"

"Why not!" laughed Will. "Those bags tied to his saddle may hold unexpected riches."

And he sprang forward and seized the horse's bridle.

The rider showed no alarm at the sight of the three men in Lincoln green. Indeed he regarded them with such a forlorn expression that Little John said, "Cheer up, Sir Knight. We are going to take you to our leader, Robin Hood. He wishes to entertain a new face to dinner. By the looks of you, you could do with a good meal."

"Robin Hood!" For a moment something like interest flickered in the knight's eyes. "Ah, yes, a worthy man indeed. My name is Sir Richard of Lea."

"Then you'll come peaceably?" asked Will.

The knight heaved a great sigh and nodded. And Much took hold of the nag's reins and led it off the highway.

Following their secret paths to the glade the three outlaws and their new acquaintance were soon back at the camp.

With a wink and a nod in the direction

of the knight's baggage, Will quickly explained to Robin Hood how they had met Sir Richard.

Robin turned to the knight whose doleful expression had scarcely changed since he had been accosted by the outlaws.

"I sent my men into the forest," said he, "to find a guest to dine with me. They have brought me you and I bid you welcome."

Sir Richard made no answer, and one of the men in Lincoln green assisted him to dismount. Then Robin, with his usual courtesy, escorted the knight to a long table under the shade of the greenwood trees. A truly magnificent spread had been prepared. But even the sight of plates piled high with roast venison and all manner of vegetables did not seem to impress the knight.

Robin and his men were soon tucking into the sumptuous meal, but Sir Richard

ate sparingly, declining, time and time again, the goblets of wine which were pressed upon him.

"Well, Sir Knight," Robin began, as the meal drew to a close. "We have fed you as handsomely as you would permit us. Now, according to our custom, I must request my good friend, Little John, to examine your baggage. If it contains gold we shall, with your permission, take it and put it to good use."

"There is nothing of value in the bags," the knight protested. "I am, good sir, as you might gather from my appearance, a knight in distress."

As he spoke, Little John was unbuckling the bags. Slowly he rolled them out on the grass, and to his dismay found only a shabby cloak and a few silver shillings.

Little John looked so downcast that Robin Hood burst out laughing. "Better luck next time!" he cried. "Now, then, Sir

Richard, if you have a tale to tell, then by all means go ahead and let us hear it."

Sir Richard hesitated, then in a sad voice he began describing his fine castle outside Nottingham and how he was in danger of losing it.

"My son, poor foolish boy," he continued, "ran into debt which he could not pay. I borrowed the money, no less than four hundred pounds, and had to mortgage my lands, my castle and all my worldly possessions to raise it."

"May I ask," interrupted Robin, "to whom you mortgaged all this?"

"To the Abbot of St Mary's at York," replied the knight, brushing a tear from his eye. "The debt must be paid in three days and I am, or rather was, on my way to confess to him that I cannot pay it."

"But surely he will not hold you to it!" cried Much indignantly.

"I am afraid he will," said the knight, "for it is known that he is a hard man and a greedy one at that! Besides, why should he not? Would it not be dishonourable on my part to fail my part of our bargain?"

Robin Hood had taken a liking to the gentle knight and he thought for a moment. Then he bade Little John go to their treasure chest and count out four hundred pounds.

When this was done, he told him to wrap the gold in the knight's second cloak and strap it once again to the horse's saddle.

Sir Richard of Lea, laughing and crying in turn, was so overcome that no matter how he tried, he could not find words to express his gratitude to the outlaws.

Robin clapped him on the shoulder, helped him don his shabby cloak and then took him to his horse. "Ride safely and fast," he said, "for York is a good distance from here and, from what you say, the Abbot will show no mercy if you fail to arrive in time."

Meanwhile, the fat Abbot of St Mary's was anxiously wondering if Sir Richard would appear on the appointed day. Sitting in his richly furnished room, he looked for all the world like a vulture waiting to swoop on its unfortunate prey.

"If he fails," he said to his clerk, "the lands, the castle and all he owns will be mine. A tidy haul indeed for the abbey!"

"By all accounts Sir Richard of Lea is a

good and honest knight," returned the clerk a shade nervously. "He deserves perhaps some pity if he cannot meet his debt."

"Pity," repeated the Abbot as if he had never heard the word before. "He will get none of this pity from me. I will still hold his lands and everything else forfeit if he is but one half penny short."

The clerk lowered his eyes, bowed humbly, and left the room. And the Abbot, who saw nothing strange in his grasping attitude, went to the cloisters. "Pity indeed," he said as he paced up and down. A gloating smile spread across his plump face as he thought of Sir Richard's fine castle outside Nottingham.

"It shall be mine!" he murmured. "It shall all be mine!"

On the day the knight was expected, the Abbot was in a fever of impatience. He had convinced himself that he would soon be in possession of great riches.

In order to make the transfer of Sir Richard's property to himself with the least possible delay he had sent for a magistrate from York to attend the interview. The necessary papers could then be drawn up, signed and witnessed on the spot.

The magistrate, a thin, sharp-featured little man, looked ill-at-ease as he entered the fine room where the Abbot sat at his polished desk. He knew why he had been

summoned and he had no wish to be party to another man's ruin.

"You won't have long to wait," said the Abbot. Then he added pompously. "Prepare your materials, my good man. I have reason to believe that Sir Richard of Lea will not be with us long . . ."

As he spoke the knight himself was announced and the Abbot greeted him with something like affection. The knight was silent as he sat down and the Abbot, after enquiring about his health, said in a business-like voice, "Now, Sir Richard, let us not waste time. Have you brought the money?" And his eyes, under their puffed lids, grew hard and wary.

"Not a penny of it could I raise," answered Sir Richard in doleful tones, and with such a gesture of despair that the Abbot could scarcely refrain from smiling.

"Excellent – er – that is to say it is with excellent forethought that I summoned the magistrate here," he burst out.

"Then I can expect no compassion, no understanding of the terrible loss I shall suffer if you hold me to the debt?" enquired Sir Richard, raising his head and staring at the Abbot.

"Certainly not!" retorted the Abbot with the greatest of firmness. "Good sir knight, you knew well the conditions when you accepted the loan. You cannot have longer to find the money and there is no question that the sum be reduced."

And once again the Abbot smiled, a gloating, triumphant smile, which showed all too clearly how he had looked forward to this moment.

At these harsh words Sir Richard rose to his feet, his eyes suddenly alight with scorn and determination.

"You will never take possession of my castle or my lands!" cried he, in a ringing voice. "It is true that I could not raise the money by my own endeavours. But I have it here – just the same."

He drew from under his shabby cloak the gold which Robin Hood had given him, and threw it down on the table.

The Abbot started, and drew a sigh of sheer disbelief. Then so great was his rage and disappointment that he began to shiver as if he were suddenly smitten with a fever. At last he made a sign and the magistrate, almost timidly, unfastened

the heavy bag and poured from it the shining gold.

"I think that you will find, my Lord Abbot, that my debt is paid right down to the very last penny," said Sir Richard quietly. "Now, gentlemen, I take my leave and I hope that I shall never see you again."

And with great dignity the knight walked to the open door, closed it gently behind him, and was soon mounted on his horse and on his way back to Nottingham. No longer did he ride like a knight in distress but as a brave conqueror, his back erect and his head held high. So happy was he at the thought of being once again master of his own fate that he broke into loud singing as he trotted along beneath the trees.

Never for a moment, however, did Sir Richard of Lea forget the man who had helped him turn defeat into victory. One day, he promised himself, one day, the gallant outlaw, Robin Hood, would truly know what it meant to have a knight at his service.

The fighting friar

AS THE months of Robin Hood's exile in Sherwood Forest lengthened into years many of his followers grew famous in their own right. Names like Will Scarlet, whose fondness for bright red stockings gave rise to his nickname, and Will-the-Wrestler and Alan-a-Dale were all known in the villages around Nottingham.

But there was one among the brave men in Lincoln green who was different from all the others. This was Friar Tuck – a tubby, immensely strong little man, almost as broad as he was tall. Few men, apart from Little John, had got the better of Robin Hood. But Friar Tuck did, and it happened like this.

One day Robin sat by the ford of a river,

which in parts ran swift and strong. He looked up and saw coming towards him an unusual figure, not very tall but with the shoulders of an ox. He was dressed in the habit of a friar with a massive wooden rosary dangling from the belt holding his robes together.

The friar's head was as round as a ball, with a bald shining crown encircled by a fringe of thick curly black hair.

In a spirit of mischief Robin called out, "Hey, reverend father, how would you like to perform your penance for the day? Carry me across this stream on your back and you will win for yourself the approval of the saints!"

The friar's small, deepset eyes under their bushy eyebrows, glinted dangerously at Robin's challenging words. He squared his shoulders and after a slight pause, announced, "My son, my master carried the weight of the world on his shoulders, shall I refuse to carry the weight of one man?"

Robin sprang to his feet and in a trice had clambered on to the friar's broad back.

Tucking up his robes, the holy man plunged into the stream and, with every step, the water rose higher and higher until it was all but touching the wooden beads of his rosary.

As if this was the signal he had been waiting for, the holy man gave a loud grunt and with a sudden heave of his massive shoulders pitched Robin clean over his head into the river.

"Now, my fully-baptised cock sparrow, it is your turn to do the honours," said the friar with a quiet chuckle as Robin, soaked through, tried to gain a foothold on the slippery riverbed.

"Why – you – you foolhardy rascal!" Robin spluttered. "For – for two pins I would . . ." Then he burst out laughing at the sight of the friar's round, perspiring face creased in the merriest of smiles imaginable.

Together they splashed their way to the opposite bank whereupon the outlaw, in the best of humours, bent his back and the friar with some difficulty, climbed upon it.

Slowly and with many a false step Robin Hood succeeded, at length, in carrying his heavy burden across the stream.

When they were both safely on the

bank, he managed to gasp, "Now, holy friar, it is your turn once again!" And he drew his sword.

To his astonishment, the friar lifted his robes and revealed that he too carried a sword, and was prepared to use it.

"On guard!" cried he.

"If you say so!" retorted Robin Hood.

They fought for a long time – each man determined to impress the other with his skill as a swordsman. Neither man, however, seemed willing to wound the other. And it fell to Robin eventually to put an end to the fight.

"Let us talk rather than fight, good father," he gasped. "You have proved yourself not once but ten times over and I salute you!"

Suiting the action to his words Robin threw down his sword and the perspiring friar, after a moment's hesitation, threw down his.

"Who are you? What brings you to the forest?" Robin asked, as they stretched out exhausted on the sweet green grass.

"I am known as Friar Tuck," answered the holy man with a broad smile.

"And I am Robin Hood," said the outlaw, grinning.

"Ah, I thought as much!" declared the friar, and his round rosy-cheeked face was suddenly aglow with pleasure. "A worthy adversary!"

"Then join me and my merry men," cried Robin. "We have need of a holy man among us, and," he added looking at Tuck's ample waistline, "I can promise you ample nourishment."

The friar was silent for a long time. Then he said in a surprisingly humble and

gentle voice, "Would I really be of use to you?"

"Indeed you would," Robin Hood assured him.

"Then I will join you," said the friar, the twinkle returning to his eyes. "But I warn you – if there are souls to be saved among your band then save them I will!"

Rising, the two men shook hands, and Robin, greatly pleased that he had found such a worthy recruit for his cause, led the way through the forest to his greenwood glade.

Not long after Friar Tuck's arrival at their camp, disaster struck! Gamwell

Hall, where Maid Marian lived, caught fire and burned to the ground. Fortunately no one died in the inferno, but Marian now had nowhere to live.

But fate ordained a happy ending. Robin asked Marian to marry him and make her home in the greenwood glade.

She came to him on a morning in spring when the air was scented with the fragrance of the forest flowers. And they were married that same evening by Friar Tuck.

Robin's heart was filled with pride and joy as he and Marian stood together under the spreading branches of the ancient oak. All around them were grouped his merry men in their suits of Lincoln green.

How hard they had worked to transform the glade into a fairyland of beauty! Garlands of flowers hung from the branches of the trees; carpets of rushes were strewn upon the grass, and the wooden huts and shelters, which had been their homes for so long, were decorated as if for some great tournament.

Never had Marian looked more beautiful as she smiled first at Robin and then at the men. In her simple dress of primrose yellow and with a garland of wild spring flowers entwined in her long hair she was a Princess in their eyes.

Friar Tuck's sermon was short and full of good humour for the holy man knew that these two young people who stood before him were truly meant for each other. And besides, the smell of roasting venison, the boiling chickens and the huge loaves of freshly baked bread were uncommonly inviting to a man of his gigantic appetite.

After the ceremony came the speeches and the toasts – the honour of the longest

speech going to Will Gamwell who had acted as best man.

No doubt Friar Tuck's blessing before the feast began was unusually brief but then it was pronounced in tones of the utmost sincerity, for he, above all men, appreciated good food. And there were smiles all round when he sat down and immediately attacked his steak.

But Robin and Marian were too happy to think about eating and, long before midnight, they stole away from that merry company so that they could be alone under the greenwood trees.

The mad butcher of Nottingham

THE SHERIFF of Nottingham continued to wage war against Robin Hood and his followers, but with little success. His failure to capture Robin irked him sorely, and there were times when he neglected his own affairs, so busy was he devising plans to capture the outlaw Chief.

The challenge to outwit the Sheriff was a great temptation to Robin and he was forever devising ways and means of getting in and out of Nottingham unnoticed.

Sometimes he told his gentle wife of his adventures and sometimes he did not. Maid Marian could shoot and hunt as well as the best of his men, and if she thought that Robin had acted in a foolhardy way, she would tell him so in no uncertain manner.

Robin was thinking about Marian's

skill with the bow as he strode along the highway in the direction of Nottingham. Marian had asked him not to go too close to town, but he was restless for adventure.

As he strode along he was presently overtaken by a plump, well-fed butcher who was on his way to the town with a cart-load of meat to sell in the market.

"Good day to you," called the butcher from the driver's seat. And he reined in his horse. "If you are going my way, young fellow, I'll be glad of your company."

The sight of the butcher gave Robin the inspiration he had been searching for.

"My good man," said he, keeping the cloak he was wearing carefully wrapped about him, "I have a mind to set up business myself in Nottingham market as a butcher. I will pay you well, not only for that horse and cart with its load of meat,

but your butcher's outfit besides."

The butcher hid his astonishment and jumping down from his cart thrust out a podgy hand for the bag of gold, which

Robin had taken out from underneath his cloak.

Then the two men went into the forest and exchanged clothes.

In his disguise as a butcher from some out-lying hamlet Robin Hood felt perfectly secure. And as he jumped on to the cart he promised his new friend that both the mare and the cart would be safely returned to him the next day.

Despite Marian's pleadings, Robin was anxious to visit Nottingham. Prince John had recently given the Sheriff more power and Robin wanted to find out how his many friends in the town were faring under the Sheriff's harsh rule.

"Besides," Robin told himself, as he reached the town and passed, without being challenged, through its gates, "it is about time I reminded my lord Sheriff that Robin Hood has not been softened by marriage."

A number of butchers had already begun to sell their meat when Robin arrived at the market-place, and he took his place among them.

Presently, in a loud voice, he began shouting, "Good folks, gather round. If you want a bargain I'm the fellow to give you one!"

Soon Robin was besieged by customers, for he charged only a penny for his steaks whereas the other butchers were charging six or seven.

News of the mad butcher spread all round the market. Even those who had come to buy vegetables could not resist the tempting bargains Robin was offering.

"He is going to ruin us," one of the rival butchers whispered to his neighbour. "We can't hope to compete with the madman!"

"He's just throwing his meat away," returned his friend. "Might as well feed the dogs with it."

By now the crowds had grown into huge proportions and as few of the other stall-holders were doing any business because of Robin, they were growing angrier and angrier.

"Send for the Sheriff!" said one of the butchers at last. "Tell him a riot is likely if he doesn't come and clear the market of this insane butcher."

Now it must be remembered that although the Sheriff had been trying for so long to take Robin Hood prisoner he had no clear idea of what the outlaw really looked like. And so, as he rode up to him now, he took him for what he seemed to be – a rather stupid butcher from some country district.

"Now then," said he, "you must pack up and go."

"Let me give your worship some of these steaks," said Robin in a slow country

accent. "I'm anxious to be rid of this meat fast so that I can hasten back to my herds."

The Sheriff, who could never resist something for nothing, graciously accepted the parcel of meat. Then another thought struck him and he said, "You mean you own a farm and herds?"

"I do," said Robin. "Big farm it is with land and the finest herds your Worship ever set eyes on."

"Why don't you dine with us at the Guild Hall?" said the Sheriff, suddenly making up his mind that there was profit to be made out of this encounter. "How many herds did you say . . . ?"

"Oh, many many!" responded the false butcher airily, "all fine horned beasts they be . . ."

That evening, as was the custom on market days, the Sheriff of Nottingham entertained all the master butchers to a grand dinner. And Robin was given the place of honour on his right.

The meal was excellent but the Sheriff, for once, did not notice what he was eating, so busy was he trying to persuade the mad butcher fellow at his side to sell his herds of cattle and his farm to him.

"I don't mind if I do," mumbled Robin at last, his mouth full of pigeon pie.

"At a fair price, of course," said the Sheriff smoothly. And he named a figure which would have bought scarcely a dozen head of cattle.

"That's not very much," said Robin doubtfully, tucking in to his venison.

"I'll pay you in gold," urged the Sheriff, "and a hundred more besides. My wife always says my generosity will be the death of me yet!"

Robin smiled grimly to himself as he accepted the Sheriff's offer, and made arrangements to meet him the next day and ride out with him to his farm.

The Sheriff was in a state of high excitement when he met Robin early the next morning, and soon they were on their way, the Sheriff on a fine prancing horse, and the 'butcher' driving his cart.

As they went at a good pace along the highway, the Sheriff began looking about him in a nervous fashion.

"What ails you, your Worship?" enquired Robin.

And the Sheriff replied, "You being a stranger to these parts may not know about the dangerous outlaw called Robin Hood. Drive on, as fast as you can, for until we are clear of the forest I won't be at ease."

"Robin Hood – did you say?" mumbled the false butcher. "Yes, I've heard of him. They say he's a fine swordsman . . ."

"Pah!" snorted the Sheriff.

"And that no man can beat him in an archery contest . . ."

"Poof!" exclaimed the Sheriff irritably. "If I could only catch him I'd have him dangling at the end of a rope in no time at all. . ."

"Ah, but first you must catch him," said Robin, trying not to smile. Then as he caught sight of a herd of deer in the distance, he shouted loudly, "Look, your Worship, would you believe it! There are some of the very herds I told you about! Are they not fine horned beasts!"

"But – but these belong to the King," stammered the Sheriff, almost swaying in the saddle in his sudden distress. "What do you mean, you stupid oaf? These are deer, not cattle, and of no account . . ."

For answer Robin Hood produced his horn, which had been hidden by his butcher's apron, and blew three short blasts. Instantly, Little John, Will Gamwell and some twenty others came bounding through the trees and on to the highway.

Before the Sheriff had time to try to escape, Robin had jumped down from the cart and grasped his mare's bridle.

"Look what a noble guest I have brought you!" he cried, a merry smile playing about his lips. "The Sheriff of Nottingham no less!"

And his men took off their caps and bowed low to the cringing Sheriff, and in such a mocking fashion that he all but fainted out of fear for his own skin.

Then Little John pulled him down from his horse as if he had been a sack of flour, and Will tied a blindfold about his eyes.

He was led, or rather half dragged, to the greenwood glade where he was speedily relieved of his gold.

Being a coward as well as a bully, the Sheriff made a shameful spectacle of himself as he began to beg piteously for his life.

"It is your own greed that has brought you here," Robin Hood told him sternly. "You thought it would be easy to cheat a poor butcher out of all his possessions."

The Sheriff began to tremble at these words for he thought his last hour had

come. But Robin suddenly laughed.

"We want nothing more from you," he declared finally. "Certainly not your miserable life! So sit down at table and enjoy the meal you have so generously paid for!"

The Sheriff made a poor show of eating and when the meal was over, submitted quietly to being blindfolded once again by Robin's men.

Little John hoisted him on to his horse and Robin led it through the forest until the highway was reached.

"Be on your way, Sheriff!" he cried, taking off the blindfold. "And remember that your greed and ambition may yet be your undoing."

News of the Sheriff's treatment at the hands of Robin Hood and his merry men was soon spread over two counties. And there was a great deal of joking and secret laughter at the Sheriff's expense.

You may be sure, however, that the Sheriff himself was never heard to speak of his dealings with the mad butcher of the market-place who had so neatly turned the tables on him.

Robin Hood to the rescue

ROBIN HOOD'S band of men now numbered close on a hundred. Three of the merriest members were brothers – Stout Will, Lester and Harry.

The brothers had grown up together and were devoted to each other and to their widowed mother who lived in a little cottage on the edge of the forest.

One morning they went out hunting with some of the other men and strayed some distance from the camp.

"Let's rest awhile," said Stout Will. "I have more weight to carry than you young striplings."

They were soon stretched out in the cooling shade of an elm tree. Suddenly, as if from nowhere, a company of foresters and swordsmen appeared, led by the Sheriff himself.

The outlaws were hopelessly outnum-

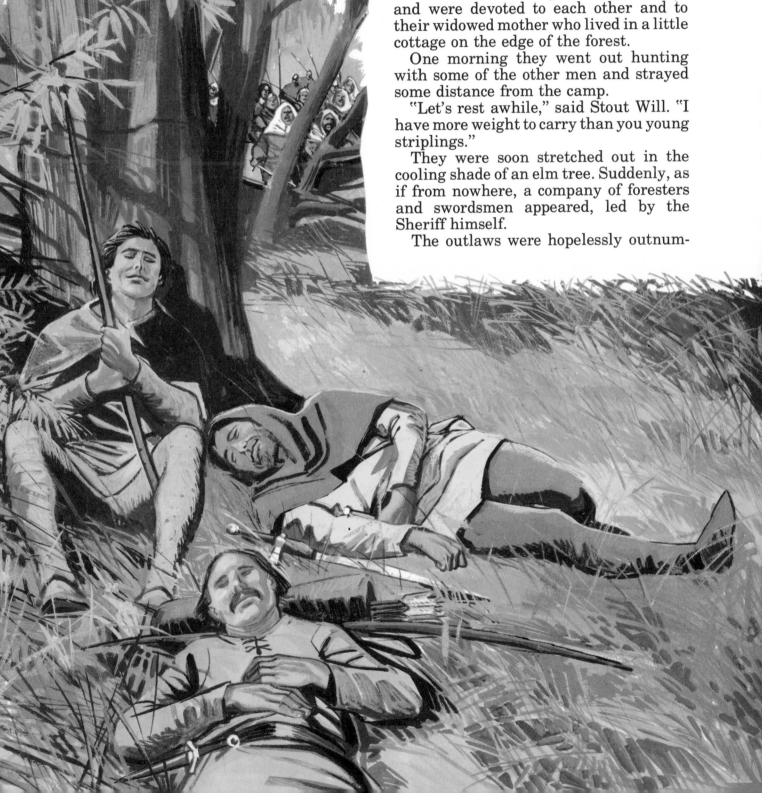

bered and took to flight. They soon out-stripped their pursuers – all except Harry, who was less nimble than the others. He lagged behind and then stumbled and fell heavily. Instantly, Will and Lester turned back to help him and were at once surrounded by a score of the Sheriff's men.

Their attackers would have killed them on the spot if the Sheriff had not shouted, "No, no, tie the rogues up and we'll take them back to Nottingham. They can rot in Jail until they dance at the end of a rope."

Robin Hood knew nothing of this until he was returning to camp. As he passed the widow's cottage she rushed out, weeping bitterly. Before Robin had time to speak, she blurted out the doleful news.

"They've taken my sons to Nottingham Jail," she sobbed. "They will be hanged for sure. Oh Robin, my poor heart is breaking at the very thought."

"Three of my bravest men at the Sheriff's mercy!" exclaimed Robin in tones of anguish. "To be hanged you say?

Never! I swear to you that it shall not be."

Robin took the weeping woman to his camp and left her there in the tender care of Maid Marian, who did her best to console the distraught widow. Then he called together his men and heard, for the first time, the whole story of the hunting expedition and the attack by the Sheriff's men.

"We must take them by surprise at the hanging," said Little John at last. "There will be huge crowds to witness it and if we disguise and arm ourselves, we can mingle unnoticed with the crowds."

"Word must be sent to Lester and his brothers," said Robin. "But the Sheriff will be expecting us to do something. I shall get in touch with them somehow. Little John, you must . . ."

After much discussion, each man knew what he was to do the next day; all except Robin. He knew he had to contact his three men but he still did not know how he was to do it.

Sleep did not come easily to him that night and he was up by daybreak and soon on his way to town, still trying to work out a way.

So deep in thought was he, as he walked along that Robin Hood scarcely noticed the beggar who was coming towards him.

"Alms, kind sir," whined the old man as he came up to Robin, "a copper or two for a poor palmer!"

Raising his eyes, Robin saw that this was no ordinary beggar. He was dressed in an old cloak covered with red and blue patches. On his head sat an immensely tall black hat which, even more than the colourfully patched cloak, told the world what he was. He belonged to an order of men who spent their lives making pilgrimages to holy places. Such men, Robin knew, were often called upon to take on the role of both priest and hangman to those condemned to die on the gallows.

An idea suddenly flashed into Robin's head.

"Come change your clothes with me," he said urgently. "Give me that high hat, your tattered old cloak, these ragged breeches and hose."

"For what purpose, sir?" asked the palmer with some dignity.

"To save the lives of three of the best men who ever lived in these parts,"

replied Robin. "And for your trouble here are six silver pieces."

The palmer did not hesitate and the exchange was soon made.

Robin, who was now in the best of spirits, whistled cheerfully until he was in sight of the town. Once he had passed safely through the gates, he strolled up and down pretending to find everything strange and interesting. The streets were already filling with people, some heading for the jail itself, others making for the market-place where the hangings were to take place at noon.

Presently, the Sheriff himself came riding down the road that led to the prison, followed by a company of his men, heavily armed. With great relief Robin noticed there was no hangman in the group. He stepped out of the crowd in front of the Sheriff's horse. The Sheriff had to rein in and angrily asked what business did the palmer have that was so urgent.

"Mighty Sheriff" mumbled the palmer. "I hear of a hanging but I see no sign of anyone in your procession to bring comfort to the souls of the poor wretches who are to die."

The Sheriff looked down from his horse in contempt. "You may indeed bring comfort and pray for their souls, but only if you will despatch them on their way. What say you, palmer, will you place the noose around their necks?"

"If the Sheriff wishes," said Robin, hiding the anger he felt rising within him. "My prayers cost nothing, my other duty shall cost . . ."

"Thirteen pence," interrupted the Sheriff. "No less, no more."

"So it shall be." said the palmer.

Some of the crowd on hearing the conversation made threatening noises at the cloaked figure. Robin heard one stout farmer declare, "If that is the man to hang three of Robin Hood's men, he shall not leave this town as easily as he entered it."

"Sheriff," cried Robin. "As part of our bargain I crave protection. Will you have your men escort me to the jail, and, after my duty is done, see me safely to the town wall?"

"See to it," said the Sheriff.

At the stroke of twelve, the gates were

thrown open and, guarded on all sides, there appeared a low cart in which stood the three brothers with halters about their necks.

Following the cart came the palmer in his high hat, one soldier on either side of him – and behind them surged a crowd of eager onlookers.

"Stand back! Stand back!" shouted the Sheriff, as the crowds surged forward into the market-place. "You will overturn the gallows!"

The Sheriff's bodyguard, using their spears and swords, cleared a space, and the three condemned prisoners were assisted from the cart and pushed and prodded forward.

As they climbed up to the scaffold the palmer came quickly after them. Now all four stood looking down on the upturned faces of the crowd, and the palmer stepped forward. A silence fell over the crowd.

"Listen to what the holy man has to say," whispered a fat housewife to her younger sister, who was now wishing she had stayed at home. "It's truly a great occasion!"

But now, strangely, the bent old palmer had suddenly straightened up. And to the astonishment of the crowd his voice rang out in the still air.

"You shall see no hangings today!" he cried in a loud strong voice. And with that he drew a hunting knife from under his rags and cut the bonds which held the prisoners. Then three short blasts from his horn rent the air.

"It's Robin Hood – the devil himself!" screamed the Sheriff in hysterical rage. "Seize him! Seize him!" he shouted to his men.

But Robin had already leapt down the scaffold steps. Behind him came Will, Lester and Harry. As they plunged into the crowd, Robin's men forced their way through the soldiers and rushed forward to meet them.

The soldiers, stunned for a moment, were slow in using their weapons and when they did, the men in Lincoln green were ready to take them on and fierce fighting soon broke out.

For a time the battle between Saxons and Normans raged fast and furious until,

once again, Robin put his horn to his lips and blew three blasts.

As one man, his followers made for the town's gates and were soon safely through. But it was not until they had reached the sheltering forest that they dared to stop and take account of those who had suffered wounds.

"I am proud of you, my bold men," Robin said, as he inspected them. And then, turning to the three brothers, he told them to hasten to the camp where their mother awaited them.

"We shall follow you more slowly," he continued, "for there are some of us here who are too battle-scarred to move very quickly."

By late afternoon Robin Hood and all his men were safely back in camp, where preparations had already been made to receive the wounded. Maid Marian tenderly bathed and bandaged the cuts and bruises, and more than a few of the injured were not too sorry that they had been wounded!

Robin watched her proudly as she moved among his faithful followers and, not for the first time, gave silent thanks that he had been blessed with such a wife.

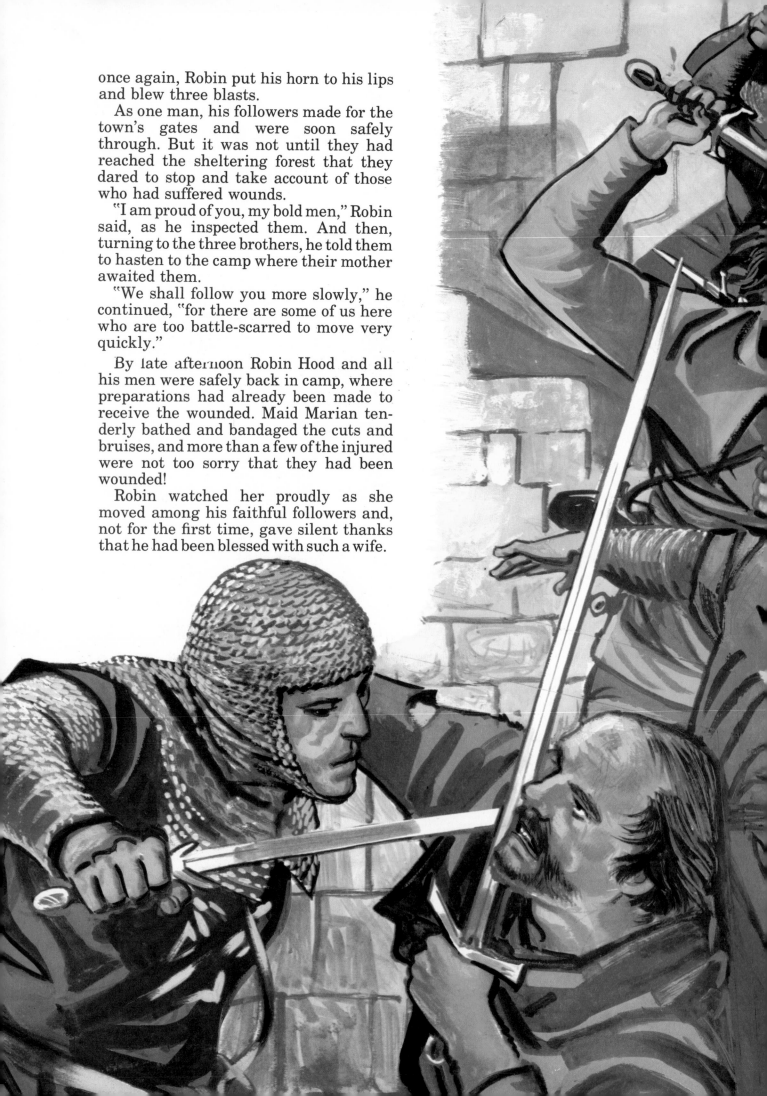

The last farewell

FOR MANY a long year, Robin and Marian lived in the forest. Robin continued to be a thorn in the Sheriff's side and Marian continued to worry about him whenever he was away from her. Her occasional anger with him, when he recounted his adventures to her, never lasted long.

One day Robin sent his men out to fetch him a guest for dinner. "Someone who will amuse me and someone who is rich so that he will not miss the payment he must make for his meal."

The guest that they brought was no ordinary knight. His clothes were fine and he bore on his chest the coat of arms of the rightful king. "Robin Hood," he declared as soon as he was brought into the camp, "I came to search for you, but your men found me first."

"You came to search for me, Sir?" said Robin. "May I ask why?" The knight stood straight and held his head high. With an air of pride he looked Robin straight in the eye. "King Richard has returned from the Holy Land and has heard of the misdeeds of his brother, John. He has also heard of you and your men. He thinks it right that

despite the fact that you have robbed him of a few of his deer, your lands and titles be returned to you. Robin Hood, I reinstate you, in the King's name, Earl of Huntingdonshire."

A great shout went up from the men. Marian rushed up and threw her arms around Robin's neck. Slightly embarrassed by such an open display of affection in front of his men, Robin eased her arms from around his neck and said, "Come, good Countess, we must prepare a special feast for the bearer of such news."

The feasting went on late into the night; happiness was tinged with sadness for the men realised that while Robin Hood could lead a band of outlaws, the Earl of Huntingdon could not. Anyway, they were no longer outlaws and were free to return to their homes and villages.

Gradually the band dispersed after Robin and Marian had left to assume their rightful place in society. Only Little John and a few others remained in the forest.

But Robin and Marian could not settle down to their new lives, and soon after returned to the forest and there lived with the remnants of the old outlaw band. They lived happily together and they grew old together. They became so close that when, after a long illness, Marian died, the sparkle went out of Robin's eyes, the chuckle went out of his voice and his shoulders became round and stooping.

Hour after hour he sat by his wife's grave beneath an ancient oak tree. And there, he was sometimes joined by faithful Little John, who could not bear to be separated from his master for long. And Little John, in an attempt to rouse his old commander, would often talk of the exploits and adventures they had shared when they were young.

But there were days, such as the present one, when nothing he said seemed of interest to his dear master. And Little John watched anxiously as, presently, Robin stretched out his hand towards the simple wooden cross. With trembling fingers he traced Maid Marian's name engraved upon the wood.

"My poor eyes are failing me, old friend," Robin said at last. "Yet I see her clearly enough . . ."

When next he spoke it was to confess to his companion that there was a dizziness in his head and a weakness in his limbs which made him feel very ill.

Greatly alarmed, Little John assisted Robin to rise.

"We must make for Kirke Hall Priory," he said urgently. "It is not so very far from here. Take my arm, old friend. I am strong enough to bear your weight."

As gentle as any woman, Little John supported Robin through the greenwood until, at last, they came to the Priory.

A young nun, on seeing Robin's condition, summoned the Abbess, who was famed for her nursing skill.

Little John carried his friend up the narrow stairs to a sparsely furnished room which looked out on the forest. Then he laid Robin down upon the couch as carefully and tenderly as if he had been a small child.

"I shall not live long," said Robin in a voice so weak that Little John could scarcely make out the words he spoke.

And before he had time to answer, the

Abbess appeared and requested Little John to leave the room so that she could administer to her patient.

The huge man sought sanctuary in the chapel where he knelt before the altar in silent prayer. But his love for Robin drew him back to the little room where his master lay, as pale as death, with closed eyes.

All that night Little John sat by Robin's couch, scarcely stirring except at the command of the Abbess who came, from time to time, to attend her patient.

Robin Hood lingered on all through the following day until the evening, when the golden light of the setting sun lit up the little room.

"Little John," he whispered suddenly. "Little John, are you there?"

"Yes, yes, I am here. I shall never leave you, master. Be sure of that!"

"I feel new strength flowing back into my limbs," Robin murmured. "Little John, did you fetch my bow? Is the horn, Marian's horn, still about my neck?"

"The horn is by your side," said Little John, "and your stout bow stands there by the window."

"Lift me up, good friend," said Robin, in a strong voice. "Lift me up and help me to the window. Then hand me the horn so that I may once again hear it echo through the greenwood."

With tears running down his furrowed cheeks Little John obeyed. Robin Hood stood, weakly swaying, at the window. Then, raising the horn to his lips, he blew one short blast.

"She will hear the sound of my horn and know that I am coming," said he, with a smile which went to the big man's heart.

"Now then, friend," continued Robin. "My bow and arrow. Give them to me and prop me up so that I may take aim through the casement."

Once again Little John did what was required of him. Robin fitted the shaft to the string and, with one last supreme effort, found strength enough to shoot it through the open window.

"Let me be buried where the arrow falls," he gasped, collapsing into his friend's arms.

"It was a fair shot, Robin!" cried Little John. "Your arrow has landed beyond the road. It has flown into the forest beneath some trees."

"Good! That was well done!"

These were the last words Little John heard his dear master speak, for almost at once Robin Hood died.

Faithful to the end, Little John did not leave the Priory until he had seen his master laid to rest. Robin Hood's grave was dug where the arrow had fallen under the trees. And beside his worn body was reverently placed his horn and his bow and arrows.

When all was done as Robin would have wished, Little John wandered away through the forest – there to make some kind of a life for himself until he too was called to his rest.